For the sake of God, may any reward
coming from this little book be
dedicated to my husband and children.

Beanie,
your goodness and strength helped write this story
and so many more - we did it sweetheart!

Prolance

www.prolancewriting.com
California, USA
©2021 Lulu Kaissi

ISBN: 978-1-7358468-7-3

Taz
in the City
• The Big Move and the Small Charity •

Written by:
Lulu Kaissi

Illustrated by:
Nouran Samy

PROLANCE

Once there was a young girl named Tasneem.
But, "Taz" was what she liked to be called.

She lived in an old house in the countryside with her mama, dad, and baby brother.

She loved this home where she had lived for as long as she could remember.

She watched the leaves on the big red oak trees change every autumn. They seemed to wave hello as they fell.

And every late spring she would pick the tiniest flowers from her neighbor's crape myrtles.

They seemed to say peekaboo as her hands met each blossom.

She would pull on her rain boots and help slippery earthworms back to the soil after a heavy rain made them lose their way.

They seemed to dance for joy in her hands.

She would zoom here and there on her scooter all around the neighborhood, feeling the wind in her hair and the sharp fresh smell of grass in her nose.

She loved growing up here. And she felt the neighborhood loved her too.

BUT, one day her parents told her that they would be moving
to a new house in the city to be closer to her dad's job!
Her parents seemed pretty excited about it.

But all of this news made Taz have a little jump in her tummy.

Over the next few months she helped pack
up the house that she loved so much.

Her bedroom, the dishes, the books, the toys...everything was put into boxes.

Before she knew it, moving day had arrived. Taz and her family all piled into the family car and got ready to follow the moving truck to the new city house.

Taz waved goodbye to her house, her trees, and all the lovely living creatures that made this place a home.

Once they arrived at her new city home, Taz noticed how different everything seemed.

She felt excited and sad at the same time. It was confusing. She sat in her new empty bedroom, staring out the window.

Soon her mama came in the room and suggested they stop unpacking and go for a walk. She handed Taz an old paper bag. "We'll pick up any garbage we see along the way, too -- just like we used to do at the old house," she said.

Taz loved cleaning up her old neighborhood with her mama. "But why do it here," she thought. "It's not the same," Taz said over the busy sounds from the street below.

"It is different here,"
her mama said. "But remember how
cleaning up helps us see things that we
may have not seen before?

And this small charity can be our way
of introducing ourselves to the living

things around us."

Taz took a deep breath
and off they went, exploring their
new neighborhood.

It was springtime and the blue jays were out calling to each other with their familiar, "jay, jay!" They seemed to be laughing at a funny joke.

As she bent down to pick up a gum wrapper, she found a family of rolly pollies underneath it. They seemed to be tumbling like little gymnasts.

Next she passed by a row of dandelions
on a patch of grass.
They were moving in the wind
as if swaying to a song.

Then she picked up four ladybugs near some crumpled paper. They seemed to be giving her hand tickly kisses.

Now that their paper garbage bags were almost full, they started walking back home.

As she arrived back to her new front step she saw the littlest bumble bee.

It seemed to say, "Tazzz."

She felt maybe she could love growing up here after all. And it could love her too.

Inspired by
the Quran and Hadith of Islam:

"There is not an animal that lives on the
earth, nor a being that flies on its wings, but they
form communities like you...Quran 6:38

"Removing a harmful object from the road is
a charity," Prophet Muhammad,
(peace be upon him) - Related by
Bukhari and Muslim.

The Author

Lulu Kaissi is an award-winning children's fiction writer- exclusive handmade awards given only to her by none other than her beloved children. When she isn't writing she fills her time homeschooling her two children, reading, process-improving, exploring nature, deepening her knowledge of Islam, and subjecting her husband to her corny sense of humor. She makes her home in Texas with her loving family, undisciplined cat, rogue legos, and piles of half-finished crochet projects.

The Illustrator
Nouran Samy is a concept artist and illustrator from Cairo, Egypt.

CPSIA information can be obtained
at www.ICGtesting.com
Printed in the USA
LVHW071626310121
677957LV00011B/397

9 781735 846873